Disclaimer

This is a work of fiction. Any names, businesses, characters, events, incidents and places are either the product of the author's imagination or used in a fictitious manner. Any resemblance to actual people, living or dead, or actual events or occurrences is purely coincidental.

Towers

By Blaine Hart

Check Out all My Books and Audio Books at:
www.LordHartRules.com

Table of Contents

Chapter 1: The Seer's Prediction

Kelyk raced up the stone steps, a few strides ahead of his younger brother. With a shout of joy he jumped the last step to the top of the tower. It had long been abandoned, but was still a mighty fortification. His father had told him many bedtime stories of soldiers that defended towers like this to help keep their land free. Pretending he had a sword in his hand, he sparred with his brother, both of them laughing as they imagined themselves to be heroes fighting off enemy invaders.

As the years went by, Kelyk ended up in the army. He was strong, tenacious, and had a charming personality that allowed him to rise to the rank of captain in a relatively short period of time. One day his commanding officer came to him with a difficult mission. He was to secure the southern border; he was to be given five hundred warriors, two hundred archers, twenty war engineers, one hundred cavalry, fifty knights, one hundred workers, and ten thousand gold pieces. It was a dangerous mission. In fact, the last five commanders and their armies where slaughtered, with only a few escaping to tell the tale. Kelyk was immediately alarmed.

"Why are you sending me to my death?" he asked, exasperated. "Think of this as an opportunity," the old warrior replied in a gruff voice. "If you can find a way to secure the southern border you will be hailed as a hero, and likely promoted to the rank of general."

"A lot of good that will do me if I'm dead!" stated Kelyk defiantly, a sneer on his lips. "Easy soldier, remember what happens to those who disobey orders. Anyway, the king himself has sent you a secret weapon to help." Grizzletooth moved in close and whispered, "We have a wizard that is to join you." Kelyk took a step back, surprise evident on his face. "Really? What types of magic does he do? How powerful a wizard are we talking? Does he take orders from me?" Grizzletooth smiled, "Yes, he will take your commands, and as for his powers, you will have to ask him yourself."

Kelyk looked up into the bright blue sky and suddenly had a feeling of confidence, as he knew just how rare wizards where in the kingdom. "Ok, I'll do it! But tell the king I need fifty catapults as well. We will teach the barbarian scum once and for all to leave our kingdom in peace!"

Grizzletooth beamed with pride and gave Kelyk a hearty slap on the back. "Now you're talking soldier! I'll let the general know the good news and see if we can get those catapults for ya!"

A few days later the order came down. They were leaving in a week and Kelyk was to meet with the top general in one hour to go over the plans. He headed to his house to freshen up and put on his best suit of armor. As he is shaving in the mirror, his mind wanders back to his childhood, to a happier time when he and his brother would play among the old towers. A slight smile crossed his lips and then he straightened up and looked dead center into the mirror, his eyes steely and glinting. "That's it!" he shouts. "I will cover the southern borders with so many towers that the enemy will quake in fear and not dare to enter our territory again!" With a sense of purpose Kelyk polished his armor and made sure his longsword was razor sharp. He then headed outside and made his way to the castle.

The sun glinted off his silver armor as he jumped onto his faithful steed and galloped towards the king's mighty castle a little over a mile away. The guards at the gate immediately let him through, and within seconds a skinny page took his horse. The war room was located in the northeast tower. After passing through several security checkpoints, Kelyk soon found himself face-to-face with the mighty general. General Vyrak is an imposing figure, standing over six and a half feet tall and covered in scars and muscle. Kelyk has heard many tales of the general's exploits; he is a living legend. Kelyk salutes then states: "Reporting for duty."

General Vyrak glares at Kelyk, a burning fire in his eyes. In a voice deep, gruff, and dangerous the general states, "The southern border has become more than an embarrassment, it is now threatening the kingdom itself. Kelyk, the king's seer has predicted that you have the greatest chance for success. She has also predicted a great tragedy for our nation if you should fail."

Kelyk squared his shoulders, "I have an idea general. With your permission and resources, I will cover the southern border in fortified towers. I know you've given me a lot already, but if you can spare ten building engineers and one hundred craftsmen, I will make the southern border a mass graveyard for our enemies."

A hint of a smile appeared on the general's face. "I have a meeting with the king tomorrow. I'll see if I can get you what you ask." The general gave Kelyk a knowing wink, and then in his gruff voice stated, "Dismissed soldier. I'll send word tomorrow." Kelyk saluted, and then headed out of the castle, his mind filled with thoughts of battle, leadership, towers, and glory.

Chapter 2: The Southern Border

Kelyk spent the next few days planning his departure to the southern border. The general was able to procure the engineers, craftsmen, and catapults requested, along with an additional one thousand gold pieces. The rest of the week was a blur of frenzied motion, as Kelyk bought all the supplies needed and made many detailed plans.

Before he knew it, the day had arrived to deploy his troops to the southern border. General Vyrak himself came to send them off. Outside of the castle gates, the general addressed the small army under Kelyk's control. "Fight for honor! Fight for glory! Fight for your country! For the last fifty years the southern border has been porous, and thousands of our people have been slain or taken captive by the barbarian scum. Their reign of tyranny needs to end. Show no mercy, and follow Kelyk's orders as if I were giving them myself. When the border is finally secure, all of you will be richly rewarded! Go now and show these barbarians what we are truly capable of!"

All assembled gave a mighty cheer. Kelyk saluted the general, turned his horse around, and shouted, "Onward to glory, the southern border awaits." With the creaking of mighty catapults, the whinnying of horses, and the clatter of men in armor, the army was on the move.

It took two weeks for the force to reach the southern border. During that time, Kelyk spent every night talking with the wizard named Marianus about his powers and abilities. What he learned delighted him. The wizard was a master earth mover, and he could quickly take huge chunks of earth and stone from any area on the ground and move it to a desired location The wizard even bragged how he buried four goblins alive at once, and how he knocked out an ogre with a large boulder. He would be quite useful in battle and in helping his troops build the fortifications and towers.

Right around mid-day of their fourteenth day of travel, the small army came to a large hill, where many of his countrymen had fought and died before. To the south the terrain got much hillier and rough with trees and dense underbrush, a total wild land. In a powerful voice, Kelyk commanded his fighting force to make camp at the top of the hill. Within hours he had his engineers, craftsmen, workers, and soldiers working along with the wizard on their very first tower. He also sent out three scouts to determine the enemy's location.

By the end of the day they were able to make a four foot tall defensive wall at the front edge of the hill, and the bottom half of the tower was complete. The wizard was amazing, just ripping the earth from the ground and placing it where needed. He was also an expert at taking out the large rocks and placing them in a pile for use by the craftsmen sand the catapult teams. Kelyk stationed some of his catapults behind the newly constructed wall, knowing that they were more vulnerable to attack now than they would ever be. There would be no fires tonight to announce their presence.

The night was uneventful and they got an early start in the morning. After only a few hours of work Kelyk heard some excited yells from the workmen. Going over to investigate, he found one of the men holding a fist sized chunk of gold in his hand. "I found it with the other rocks milord." Kelyk's eyes grew with excitement, "Good work soldier, I'll find a good use for this. Your main job from now on is to find any gold you can and bring it to me." Kelyk held out his hand and the soldier quickly gave him the gold nugget and saluted, "Yes captain!"

By lunch time one of the scouts had returned. He had spotted the barbarians fifteen miles to the south and they were headed this way. The other scout had stayed behind to count their numbers and keep an eye on them. With this new information, Kelyk got his force to work at an even more frenzied pace, and by the end of that day their first tower was complete and surrounded by a five foot tall earthen wall, courtesy of the wizard. The tower was a basic design standing ten feet wide and twenty foot tall, with enough room to hold a lot of his men. The area was also rich in gold, as Kelyk had a small sack full of gold nuggets already.

Another night of cold rations for the soldiers - the element of surprise was too valuable to give up for the warmth and comfort of a fire. At midnight his second scout returned. He reported a fairly large contingent of over five hundred barbarians camped just five miles away - probably on their way to terrorize the southern villages once again. They were sure to discover their position tomorrow.

Kelyk had trouble sleeping through the night. His mind raced over dozens of strategies to best prepare for their first battle. He did manage a few hours of sleep, however, and woke up at the crack of dawn, barking orders immediately.

He had decided to reinforce their position and disguise his troop strength in hopes that the barbarians would underestimate him. He also summoned his best scout and gave him the sack of raw gold ore recently excavated. His orders were to head west to the coastal city of Hyruk and hire as many mercenaries as possible along with fresh supplies for the army.

The scout left immediately on one of the fastest horses, as the village was around a week away. The rest of the day was a blur. Kelyk sent out a small hunting force to gather as much food as possible, while everyone else fortified their position, sharpened their weapons, and prepared for battle.

Several hours after noon the last scout appeared, galloping toward their base. He immediately has to slow down when he gets closer to avoid the various ditches and walls his soldiers, workers., engineers, and wizard had recently constructed. He rushed up to Kelyk and stated, "My Lord, the barbarians will soon be upon us. They are marching this way and should spot us within the next several hours." Kelyk smiled, "Good job soldier, go ahead and grab some food, then prepare to defend our position." Kelyk motioned towards the tower and the scout saluted and headed off.

The next few hours are a frenzy of motion as Kelyk has the earth wizard make several more large piles of stones for use in their catapults. He makes sure every single catapult is loaded and can be quickly fired upon command. He also took most of his fighting force and hid them in the tower, and behind the tower, hoping to draw the barbarians in. He had also positioned the cavalry about a five minutes ride away behind another hill and out of sight.

It wasn't long before long the enemy was spotted coming out of the ravine to the south. Kelyk could hear the barbarians yelling amongst themselves from nearly half a mile away. After several minutes they were on the move again, jogging now and heading right towards them.

Kelyk had placed some of the workers on the hill as bait, with no shirts, no weapons, and pretending not to notice the barbarians. When the barbarians were within two hundred yards of the fortifications they started screaming battle cries and rushing at the frightened workers. The workers played their role well, waiting until the last second to rush up the hill and get behind the wall for safety. Kelyk pulled out his war horn and sounded it mightily. This is the signal for the Calvary to head out of their hiding place and circle behind the enemy to hit them in the rear, as well as the signal for the catapults and archers to open fire. Within seconds the fifty catapults are flinging rocks through the air, while his two hundred archers send off volley after volley of arrows. The barbarians are caught off guard but still keep running forward, despite losing many of their numbers to the deadly barrage. When the barbarians reach the base of the hill and their defensive wall, Kelyk blows his war horn again. The door to his tower flies open and a steady stream of his warriors and knights come out of hiding. Kelyk draws his own sword and fights with his men at the wall surrounding the hill.

The barbarians are ferocious fighters and extremely strong and brave. Many are able to climb over the wall at the southwestern corner, and the bloodshed there is immense. The wizard Marianus, however, is able to use his powers to temporarily heighten the wall and halt the flow of the attackers, allowing his knights the time to rally and push them back..

With half their force decimated in such a short period of time, the barbarians quickly retreat. Kelyk's archers and catapults inflict many additional casualties as they run away. The remaining barbarians rush back to the south and for the safety of the ravine. The Calvary catches them totally by surprise, cutting them off. It is a massacre, with only a few escaping. It is a glorious victory, with his force only sustaining twenty fatalities and a variety of minor injuries compared to the nearly five hundred barbarian bodies that lay strewn across the battlefield. Kelyk had hoped to kill or capture them all, as now the element of surprise was gone. Now is when the true test will begin, as the barbarian numbers are rumored to be in the thousands or tens of thousands, and they would not be happy to hear what the survivors tell them.

Kelyk gave his workers the gruesome task of searching the dead for any valuable items, weapons, or armor. He then had the earth wizard use his magic to dig a massive hole in the earth to bury the enemy dead. He then buried his own men in a sunny field behind the tower. After giving them a proper burial and bandaging up the wounded, he gathered up his men for a quick meeting.

When everyone is assembled, he congratulates them on their victory. "Now don't get too cocky, for when they return they will bring an army twenty times the size of the force we faced today. By my estimations, we will have two to three weeks before they are again upon us. I have summoned some reinforcements who should be here within the next two weeks. If we are to survive and hold this border, we are going to need to build as many towers as possible. With the help of our mighty earth wizard Marianus, we will connect each tower with ten foot high walls that we can walk across. That way we can reinforce our positions quickly. Over the next two weeks we will need at least four more towers completed, one on each corner of this hill. If we can withstand the next assault, we will be in a great position to hold the border for as long as we live and receive a generous reward from the king. I know I ask a lot of you, but the safety and security of our kingdom lies with us. Failure will leave us vulnerable to attack for decades to come, if we even last that long. Now get to work, for honor, glory, and our kingdom!" The men cheer mightily and then head off to their respective tasks.

Chapter 3: Heroes

The next week goes by smoothly. There is lots of wildlife from the forests and streams nearby to help supplement their rations. His army is in a good mood and the four towers are being built at a great pace. Kelyk was able to report the good news of his first victory to a messenger sent by the king. But before the messenger left the camp, he handed him a large sack of gold ore from their most recent excavations, hoping the king would send him some more troops and supplies in return. Kelyk also sent several scouts deep into enemy territory to keep an eye on the barbarian's troop movements.

After two weeks the four towers were completed, and the very next day his most trusted scout Ramsin returned with three hundred mercenaries from the coastal city of Hyruk. Kelyk spent the whole day with the new mercenaries, getting to know them and finding out how much training they've already had. Most of them claim to be fishermen, but Kelyk knows that many are pirates or have been at one point in their lives. They are well armed, mainly with swords and daggers, and with light armor, mostly leather. Ramsin also introduces him personally to three heroic looking figures, all of them with unique magical talents. Nearly half of the gold was spent on just these three, but Kelyk knows that magic has swayed the tide of many a battle.

One of the heroes is named Vlad, a mighty paladin who wears shiny steel plate mail armor and wields a golden mace with a golden shield. Kelyk has heard of this hero before, rumored to be blessed by the gods with the ability to heal the wounded. It has also been said that anyone around him in battle is granted extra strength and courage. Kelyk can't believe his luck to have found this holy warrior, if it was luck at all and not some divine providence that he did not understand.

The other hero is dressed in leather and fine silks. His name is Margyn, and Kelyk has heard of him as well. He carries with him a small drum, a lute, and a flute. His music is said to be magical, with the ability to charm his enemies and bring courage and joy to his allies. He and Vlad were good friends.

The third hero, if you can consider a witch a hero, stands over six feet tall with long gray hair and a wrinkled face. She claims to be able to make magical potions of all sorts that will be helpful on the battlefield, as well as commanding some darker magic to instill fear and chaos amongst the enemy. Her name is Crowlyn, and she is rumored to be hundreds of years old, a permanent resident of Hyruk as long as anyone can remember. She also has the unsettling habit of cackling loudly to her-self every so often, making those around her nervous.

After all the new recruits and heroes have been given their roles in the upcoming battle, it's back to improving the defenses. Two days later a scout returns with news of the enemy's movements. The news is not good, but is expected. A massive barbarian horde is on the way, too many for the scout to count. It also appears that they have some siege weapons, which is bad news indeed. The scout estimates they have approximately four days before the group is upon them.

With the news of such a large force with siege weapons on the way, Kelyk triples the amount of hunters and gatherers to store up their food and water supply. Kelyk also makes sure that they have a massive array of stones for the catapults and that the archers have hundreds of extra arrows. Kelyk has always loved the bow and arrow as a weapon. He was lucky enough to have two hundred of the nation's best archers, many of whom he had trained personally. With the protection and height of the towers, they were possibly his greatest asset. Kelyk had stayed with the soldiers on the ground in the first battle, but from now on he was going to be giving commands from the towers, his bow in hand.

The next three days went by quickly. The hunters and gatherers were able to gather several weeks' worth of surplus food in case of a siege. Kelyk had ordered all the soldiers to restrict their activities to just a few hours of training a day. He wanted them fresh and strong for the upcoming battle. The next morning, his last two scouts come galloping into camp pursued by over fifty barbarians on horseback. A few of them were able to throw some spears at the scouts; a few came close but none hit their mark, and the barbarians quickly retreated after a few alert soldiers lobbed some large rocks at them from their catapults.

The scouts immediately reported to Kelyk that the Army was just a few miles away. They looked scared when describing the huge force that was coming. One of the scouts mentioned a massive barbarian riding a black stallion that was surrounded by many fierce looking warriors in war paint. Kelyk surmised that this was likely the leader of the enemy army. After getting the full report from his scouts, Kelyk headed to the orange tent inhabited by the old witch Crowlyn.

Just as Kelyk was about to announce his presence, the tent flap opened, allowing a large plume of smoke to escape and revealing the old woman holding a glowing green staff topped with the skull of some sharp toothed beast. Crowlyn cackles, sending a slight shiver down Kelyk's spine. Seeming to read his mind, Crowlyn stated with a glint in her eye, "Ready for me to make my battle potions?" Kelyk nodded his head, "Yes, and anything else you can do to help us win this battle will be greatly appreciated."

The old woman looked quite different today to Kelyk. She almost seemed to shimmer with some kind of unknown power that gave him the creeps. She then cackled again and stated, "I've got an extra special brew in store for you. I've perfected the recipe over the last few decades, and with all the trouble the barbarians have caused to the people of my city, it's time for them to pay the price." She then lifted her arms into the air holding her staff high and mumbling under her breath. Her staff began to glow brightly and then she started yelling out orders to a group of five younger-looking witches who come out of the tent dragging a massive black cauldron.

As the day progressed, the full might of the barbarian army became apparent. There were thousands upon thousands of them, and throughout the rest of the day they surrounded Kelyk's hill top fortress totally.

A few unlucky barbarians got too close and were killed by several well aimed shots from the catapult crew. The barbarians soon learned the range of the catapults and stayed well back. Kelyk's army was completely surrounded, and right before sunset the barbarian artillery started lobbing boulders at them. Kelyk's soldiers were ready, however; with a catapult on top of each tower. It didn't take long before they had destroyed the five poorly made artillery pieces of the barbarians, with little damage done to their defenses. The soldiers gave out a great cry of victory as the barbarian's last siege weapon was blown to pieces by a well-aimed boulder.

That night the countryside was filled with blazing bonfires everywhere Kelyk looked. He doubled the guards on the towers in case of a night attack and made sure that everyone had a good meal so they would be ready for battle in the morning. Kelyk couldn't be sure that they would attack tomorrow, but his gut was telling him that they would. Before heading to bed, Kelyk met with his officers, his wizard Marianus, the witch Crowlyn, and the paladin and bard Vlad and Margyn. He assigned Vlad and Margyn to his knight's squadron, their job to make sure the barbarians didn't breach their defenses, and if they did, to kill them as soon as possible. Unfortunately, Marianus was exhausted from his weeks of earth moving, but he assured Kelyk he still had a few tricks up his sleeve. He gave his five officers a different location to defend, and warned them that if things got really bad, they were to retreat to the main tower in the center of the base, the largest and most defensible asset they had.

Crowlyn had been quite busy and had prepared two massive batches of potions for use by the army. She had created enough battle elixir for each and every soldier, said to give incredible strength, increased dexterity, and heighten awareness. She also created many healing potions for anyone wounded in the battle.

Just as the last plan had been set and Kelyk was about to go to bed, Crowlyn cackled gleefully, "I have a rather unpleasant surprise for our enemy tonight as they sleep." Kelyk nodded to her and stated, "We appreciate your help." Kelyk made one last roundabout of the defenses, then headed to bed, his armor, bow, and sword nearby in case of a night assault.

Kelyk had only been sleeping a few hours when he was awakened by an eerie sound and the shouts of the soldiers. He grabbed his sword and rushed outside to see what was going on. In the middle of the camp he saw Crowlyn and her apprentices holding hands and chanting around a large bonfire with blue flames. The eerie noise he had heard was coming from the flames themselves. Rubbing his eyes, Kelyk looked at the flames again, seeing what looked like hundreds of ghost-like figures dancing in the flames. His soldiers looked terrified and ready to strike at the witches, but Kelyk shouted loudly, "Hold your weapons!" And his soldiers immediately fell back. The old crone had promised Kelyk a surprise, and apparently this was it.

Kelyk watched for several more minutes as the witch and her assistants began to chant and dance about the flames more feverishly. Then suddenly a god-awful sound like that of an entire village being snuffed out howled from the blue flames as thousands of dark apparitions poured out of the bonfire and into the night sky towards the surrounding barbarian army.

Kelyk rushed to the southeast tower and sprinted up the stairs to the top. Looking out, he couldn't see much except the many bonfires scattered across the landscape, but even from this far away he could hear the screams and cries coming from the barbarian's various campsites. It was over an hour before some semblance of order was brought to the barbarian campsites, and Kelyk could no longer hear them screaming.

Not wanting to start the next day un-rested, Kelyk headed back to his quarters to try and get a few more hours of sleep. He looked for Crowlyn on his way to thank her for help, but she was nowhere to be seen. When Kelyk finally did make it to his quarters, he found it very difficult to sleep; the inhuman howling and ghost images kept running through his mind. Eventually he did fall asleep for a few hours, only to be awakened at the break of dawn by one of his commanders. "My Lord, the barbarians are massing, you must make ready." Kelyk jumped out of bed and quickly put on his armor, grabbed his sword and bow, and headed outside.

Most of his troops were awake and preparing for battle, but for those who weren't, he pulled out his war horn and blew it mightily. Near the center of camp Kelyk saw Crowlyn and her apprentices stirring a massive black cauldron. He walked up to them and was greeted by the old witch who smiled, revealing her stained and crooked teeth. "That was quite a show you put on last night," stated Kelyk. "I appreciate all your help." The old witch cackled. In a raspy voice she said, "They will be attacking today. My spirits put a terrible fright in them, and they will be too spooked to sit idle for another day. I've got one last present for you."

Crowlyn took a wooden cup and dipped it into the cauldron and handed it to Kelyk. Not wanting to offend her, Kelyk downed the potent and bitter brew in three mighty swallows. He immediately shook his head and resisted the urge to spit. It was not long before a sense of euphoria and strength enveloped him. Everything around him seemed more colorful, and his movements were effortless and graceful. "I really like it," stated Kelyk, giving her a genuine smile. "I've got enough for everyone; I used up five years' worth of herbs in this one batch. Have your men line up for their medicine." Kelyk nodded and thanked Crowlyn again. After filling his water skin with the potent brew, Kelyk gave his war horn a mighty blast and ordered his soldiers to get in line and drink the magical potion.

Chapter 4: The Horde

After everyone has had their breakfast and a swig of Crowlyn's battle elixir, Kelyk had everyone head to their defensive positions. The soldiers were brimming with excitement, the potion definitely having an effect on them. In the distance the booming of drums could be heard, a menacing sound. Kelyk headed to the north-east tower and took his position on top at the very front, near a catapult and six barrels filled to the brim with arrows. He took a few practice shots with his mighty bow to gauge the distance, and then settled back and watched the movements of the barbarian horde.

Nothing much happened for several hours save the incessant drumming. Then suddenly the drum beats got louder and Kelyk saw the barbarian army start to move forward as one. He gave a mighty blast on his war horn, and he could hear the other soldiers signaling the advance of the barbarians as well. They were moving in from all sides all at once.

Within minutes the horde was in range of their catapults, and large rocks began flying through the air, causing some serious damage. Not long after that, they were within range of the archers, and Kelyk began shooting as many arrows as he could at the incoming army from his tower fortress. The barbarians were now running at the walls, some of them carrying large ladders while others were using grappling hooks to try and scale the walls.

At this close range Kelyk was wreaking havoc with his bow. There were so many barbarians that it almost seemed impossible to miss. The enemy were taking tremendous casualties but continued to press onward. A few made it over the defenses, but Kelyk wasn't worried about that at the moment. He had his knights, Calvary, mercenaries, and soldiers waiting for them. He was in a rhythm now, his bow string snapping every two seconds. The catapult next to him continued to fire, and when at last the enemy was too close to the towers and walls to fire upon, the catapult crew brought the stones to the wall and dropped them on the heads of the enemy below.

In the distance something weird caught Kelyk's eye. He saw several humanoid shapes with black robes waving their arms over several dead soldiers. Not wanting to be distracted for too long, Kelyk scanned the nearby wall and immediately fired his bow at an invader on a ladder nearly at the top of the wall. His aim was true, and the man screamed as he plummeted to the ground below. Kelyk fired off several more shots in a row, not allowing anyone else to get up the ladder. Taking a second to look into the distance, he saw the three dark robed men chanting and waving their hands over what looked like more dead bodies. It was shocking when he noticed those bodies rise from the ground and start walking towards the battlements. With a fright, Kelyk remembered several stories he had heard from two drunk soldiers who had survived the last failed attempt by the king to keep the southern border secured. They had told him with fear in their eyes how the dead would rise and attack them with glowing red eyes.

The loud noise of several of his soldier's war horns immediately pulled Kelyk's attention to the inside quarter of their defenses. The Western wall was being overrun, and barbarians were coming over in large numbers. Kelyk stood and ordered his five best archers, who he had trained personally, and who always stayed next to him in battle, "Grab two barrels of arrows and follow me!" His archers quickly obeyed and followed Kelyk from the tower and onto the top of the wall that stretched to the north-western tower. The six moved quickly, easily dodging a few spear and ax throws. The barbarians used very few ranged weapons, a massive advantage his army had that he was exploiting.

A little over halfway to the northwestern tower, Kelyk and his archers encountered a group of fifty barbarians attempting to sneak over with ladders and grappling hooks. Knowing that he could not leave them to attack him from behind, Kelyk grabbed his bow from his back and ordered his men to quickly open fire. Kelyk's first shot was sloppy and fell short. His hand instinctively went to his waist and his extra-large water skin filled with Crowlyn's battle elixir. He quickly took a mighty swig and then quickly corked it and lined up his next shot. This time his arrow flew true, sinking deep into the side of a leather-clad barbarian that was halfway up the wall. With his bodyguard of archers firing off six arrows every few seconds, it took them less than a minute to kill many and send the rest running for cover. Kelyk pulled out his war horn and blew it mightily, to let the men on the western wall know that reinforcements were on the way.

The screams and shouts from the western wall give further urgency to Kelyk as he ran across the top of the wall to the wood and steel door guarding the upper entrance to the tower. An alert soldier immediately opened the door, allowing Kelyk and his men to rush inside and up the stairs to the top of the tower. At the top, he made his way to the western edge and scanned the situation. There were over ten ladders filled with barbarians climbing to the top of the walls. He also saw many men on grappling hooks pulling themselves to the top. Glancing downward inside his defenses, he saw his knights, soldiers, and Calvary fighting ferociously. Kelyk immediately shouted, "Full fire on the ladders and grappling hooks." He knew instinctively that he needed to stop the flow of barbarians into the courtyard as quickly as possible.

Kelyk pulled out his mighty longbow again and let loose. The next fifteen minutes passed by in a blur of motion, the witches potion allowing him to perform at peak performance. He had already lost count of the number of men who had been hit by his arrows. Hundreds of barbarians lay at the base of the wall, most dead from arrows or the fall. He noticed the remaining barbarians had retreated out of bow range and were headed toward the southern wall.

The blast of his knight's distinctive war horns caught Kelyk's attention. Despite stopping the flow of barbarians into the courtyard, hundreds of the horde were still fighting inside the fortress. They were ferocious in hand-to-hand combat and were striking many killing blows to his men and mercenaries.

Kelyk quickly signaled for his five elite archers and ten of the nearest archers to follow him, ordering them to refill their barrels with arrows from the various stockpiles around them. He quickly dashed down the stairs to the ground level, took a quick look through the small window of the stout wooden door, and seeing the coast was clear, he unlocked it and rushed into the large central courtyard. Quickly surveying the battlefield, he could see his knights and what looked like Vlad in his gleaming silver armor fighting ferociously with a large group of barbarians. They were several hundred yards away, so after taking another large swig of the magical elixir, Kelyk rushed toward the battle with his archers right behind him.

As he got closer he could hear what sounded like a beautiful lute playing a well-known battle song. The rousing tune invigorated Kelyk even further, and when he and his archers had gotten within fifty yards of the ferocious battle, he grabbed his bow and started firing. He was careful to pick and choose his targets, and if one of his own soldiers was too close he would search for a better target. He had several brilliant shots, one of them an arrow that caught a massive barbarian in the neck; sending him to the ground gurgling blood.

It was not long before the carnage they were causing brought a large group of over twenty barbarians charging their way. Kelyk got one more hurried shot off, catching a barbarian in the shoulder, before he slung his bow across his back and drew his long sword. Three of his elite archers and the other archers draw their swords, while his two best elite archers ran to a better position and opened fire with their bows once again.

As the barbarians charged in, the first thing Kelyk noticed before they were upon him was just how incredibly large they were. He jumped to the left as a massive barbarian drove an over-head battle axe into the ground where he was just standing. Quickly, Kelyk grabbed his long sword with both hands and swung mightily at the barbarian's exposed neck, sending his head sprawling and covering Kelyk in blood. Another barbarian with a look of absolute hatred on his face swung a mighty spiked club at Kelyk. He barely ducked under the blow and drove his longsword into the barbarian's belly at the same time as an arrow shot into the barbarians right arm. The barbarian, adrenaline pumping through him, immediately swung his spiked club at Kelyk, this time landing a mighty blow to Kelyk's head. Unfortunately, Kelyk's helm was made of chainmail and leather and not plate, and he fell into unconsciousness.

The next thing Kelyk remembered seeing was the barbarian warrior lying dead on the battlefield; one of his loyal soldiers had pierced the barbarian in the heart with an arrow. It was odd, though, because he was looking down on the scene as if he was on one of his towers, and the body next to the slain barbarian sure looked like his own. Then a blinding white light caught his attention: looking above him he saw what looked like a magnificent castle made of crystal shining with all the colors of the rainbow. Looking closer, he could see people waving at him, and the more he concentrated on the light and the castle, the closer he got to it and the more magnificent it became. Just as he was getting within shouting distance, he suddenly found himself dragged back down to Earth at an incredible speed.

The next thing he knew he was staring into the glowing blue eyes of Vlad, with unbelievable pain on the left side of his head. The mighty paladin raised his fist in the air, which began to glow brightly, then touched Kelyk on the head where the barbarian's club had hit. Kelyk felt the pain immediately disappear and he stood up, noticing the concerned looks from several of his elite bodyguards. Surveying the carnage around him, he immediately thanked the paladin, who gave him a quick salute and then rushed off towards the southeastern tower where several war horns could be heard blasting for reinforcements.

Still feeling a bit woozy and seeing only five of his archers left standing, Kelyk turned to the closest soldier, and asked, "How long was I out? What are the damages?" He laid a hand on Kelyk's shoulder, "Glad to see you alive! Thought you were dead for sure! If we live through this you ought to double that paladin's pay, he saved your life for sure." Then with a sad expression he stated, "You were out for at least fifteen minutes. It was all I could do to keep them off of you. It's just the five of us left, and we would be dead too if Vlad, Margyn, and several of our knights hadn't of come to the rescue." Kelyk looked at the remaining soldiers, three of them his elite archers, and one of them a mighty knight ordered to stay back and make sure their commander survived the battle. Kelyk grabbed his water skin and drank the last of his battle elixir, pausing a moment to clear his head. He then pointed towards the southeast tower and started marching, "This way men!"

Chapter 5: Dark Magic

Still feeling a bit dizzy, but getting better with each step, Kelyk stopped close to the tower and shot off a barrage of arrows at a small group of invaders who had just scaled the top of the wall. With the help of his trusted men, they were soon no longer a threat. Kelyk jogged the rest of the way to the tower and banged his fist on the door, commanding the soldiers inside to open it. The door opened soon enough, and Kelyk climbed to the top of the tower, his legs burning with exertion. Once he reached the top he quickly scanned the battlefield. Dead bodies were everywhere, but his attention was drawn to the right, where large contingents of his forces were fighting atop the wall against a surge of enemy forces. He could hear Margyn's magical song and could see Vlad in his silver armor fighting ferociously with his knights and soldiers around him.

Kelyk filled his quiver with fresh arrows and then he and his other archers opened fire on the encroaching horde below. After several minutes Kelyk noticed that although his arrows were finding their mark, the enemy combatants were not falling. It was getting late in the day now, and the Sun was about to set. Something was happening off in the distance; Kelyk could see the dark robed men standing back beyond bow range and waving their hands in the air, bringing even more dead to life. He knew his men were getting exhausted and that a second army of undead would eventually overrun them. He needed to kill those evil wizards immediately. Scanning the courtyard he saw the majority of his Calvary backing up Vlad and his knights as they guarded the wall.

Kelyk barked a swift order for everyone to follow him, and then rushed down the steps and into the courtyard. Once there, he jogged to the nearest mounted soldier and ordered him to dismount. He jumped on the horse and quickly galloped to the Calvary commander, "Gather your troops and meet me at the southeast tower." The commander saluted and began barking orders to his men.

Kelyk kicked his horse into a gallop and made his way to the central tower. Once inside, he headed down to the secret chamber where Marianus was staying. Kelyk burst into the small room, waking the exhausted wizard. "Marianus, I know we've taxed your powers to the limit in helping us create these defenses, but I need you now or all is lost." Marianus climbed out of bed and grabbed his staff. "I am at your service."

The two quickly exited the tower to find seventy cavalrymen waiting for them at the south eastern tower. Kelyk jumped on his horse and galloped to them. "The enemy wizards are bringing the dead back to life. If we are to survive, we must kill them. You will know them by the black robes that they wear." Kelyk shouted as he pointed to the South. "Marianus, please grant us passage." The old wizard nodded his head and started chanting in a deep guttural tone while making mystical movements with his hands. A five foot gap in the wall began to appear. It took several minutes and most of the wizard's remaining strength to create the breach. Once the Calvary had made it beyond the wall, Kelyk grabbed a lance from a nearby soldier, then blew his war horn mightily and pointed towards the dark robed figures in the distance, "CHARGE!"

Kelyk was immediately in the lead, but it was not long before many of his best riders had overtaken him, their lances at the ready. A few barbarians tried to intercept their group, but on foot they had little chance.

As the sun began to wane, they closed to within one hundred yards of the evil wizards. They were not alone; the wizards were surrounded by at least one hundred skeletons and undead warriors. Kelyk noticed the three wizards starting to chant furiously as he was closing in, and then his attention shifted to the mangled body of an undead barbarian before him. His lance hit him straight in the heart, knocking it to the ground. His other troops were wreaking havoc, their swords and lances dealing devastating blows. Seeing a slight opening, Kelyk drew his longsword and charged through the undead toward the wizards.

Several of his men were having great difficulty, with a few horses running away in fright or bucking loose their riders. Up ahead, Kelyk saw dark smoke rising around the three wizards, and then a terrible a howl pierced the battlefield as a black demon took form. It was covered in black scales with huge muscled arms, clawed hands, and a massive mouth filled with razor sharp teeth.

Slicing off the head of the nearest skeleton, Kelyk quickly sheathed his sword and grabbed his trusty longbow. He had a clear view, and fired off three arrows in rapid succession. All three hit their mark, piercing the largest dark robed wizard in the neck and twice in the chest. He collapsed, and at the same hundreds of undead collapsed from all over the battlefield.

Kelyk suddenly felt a jabbing pain in his leg. He instinctively kicked his horse forward, pushing a large zombie with a crooked helm away from him, it's dagger covered in his blood. He no longer had a clear shot at the other wizards, so he quickly galloped to the left where he saw an opening. After fifty yards he sees his chance and lines up his bow with another of the dark wizards. Out of the corner of his eye he sees one of his men being torn to shreds by the large demon. With a chill down his spine, Kelyk focuses on the task at hand and fires off multiple shots. Most of them miss their mark, but one hits the dark necromancer in the belly, and that was all the distraction needed for one of his alert soldier to charge forward through five undead and chop off the necromancers head. Even more of the undead crumble to the ground throughout the battlefield without their master's magic to keep them moving.

The last Wizard had surrounded himself with the remaining undead, making him a very difficult target. That doesn't a deter Kelyk, however, as he shoots arrow after arrow in his general vicinity. His men were now openly running from the demon, as anyone who got too close was getting killed quite savagely. With a renewed sense of urgency, Kelyk kept on firing, and then, as the sun was almost gone below the horizon, the remaining undead collapsed. One of his arrows must have hit its mark. All that was left was the black demon and about thirty of his Calvary.

Not too far away Kelyk saw several hundred barbarians running towards them. Kelyk quickly sounded his war horn, the tone for retreat, and galloped with his remaining men back to the breach in the wall. As soon as they were all safely inside the courtyard, the exhausted earth wizard began piling earth and stone to repair the hole in the wall. Meanwhile, Kelyk blew his war horn furiously, calling for reinforcements. It only took a few minutes for sixty of his knights led by Vlad and Margyn to come to their aid. Marianus was able to repair the wall up to five feet before he collapsed in exhaustion. Kelyk rushed to the Wizard and slung him over his shoulder, and then made his way to the nearby tower.

Once inside, he laid him down next to the guard at the door, and then started climbing the stone steps that lead to the top. He is exhausted when he at last reached the top of the tower. It was manned by six archers who were wreaking havoc on the barbarians below. Kelyk quickly refills his quiver and begins firing as well, his fingers swollen and bleeding. Any barbarian that made it through the breach was quickly cut down by the mighty paladin and Kelyk's loyal knights. As the last of the sunlight leaves the land, the remaining barbarians retreat. Kelyk puts every eligible soldier that isn't too wounded or exhausted on guard duty. He knows by the wholesale slaughter that the barbarians would not be able to mount another assault, but the demon was still out there, and that thing truly frightened him.

Kelyk did not sleep at all that night; he spent most of his time with his officers, commanders, and his hired heroes. Margyn kept up morale through the night next to a mighty bonfire while singing magnificent songs of glory and battle. Kelyk thanked Vlad personally for saving his life, promising him a huge reward. The old witch Crowlyn was especially gleeful and quite happy. She gave him several brews that made him forget about sleep and that helped take away his pain. He told her all about the demon, and she reassured him that she had a magic charm that she could use to trap it. She told him that once the evil wizards were slain, the demon was set loose to follow its own desires. She promised to hunt it down first thing in the morning before it got too far away.

When the morning finally came, the unbelievable carnage is mind-boggling. Kelyk had lost half of his forces, but they had easily killed the majority of the attacking barbarians, easily ten kills for every one of their dead. Crowlyn had given the wizard Marianus a mighty batch of restorative potion so he would have the strength to bury the dead, and Vlad was able to use his holy powers to resurrect a few of his favorite fallen comrades. Then, with a group of ten of his best knights, Vlad, the bard, and the witch headed out to hunt the demon, a fist sized ruby streaked with black veins in Crowlyn's hand.

Kelyk sent out scouts to track the retreating enemy's movements and then proceeded with the grim task of looting and then burying the dead. It took several days before some sense of normalcy returned. Crowlyn returned victorious, with quite a story told by the bard Margyn about their ferocious battle with the demon, eventually weakening it enough for Crowlyn to trap it inside her magical ruby prison.

A few days after that, two hundred soldiers from the king arrived. Although they missed the battle, Kelyk put them to work making their fortress bigger and stronger. He also sent a messenger to the king reporting their victory.

Chapter 6: Legacy

A month after their victory all the hired mercenaries had returned to their homes. Kelyk gave Vlad and Margyn a huge sack of gold ore each from his new gold mine. Vlad vows to use some of the gold to help an impoverished village over the sea.

The barbarians had retreated deep into their own country and showed no signs of coming back. The King was overjoyed with news of his victory and gave Kelyk the rank of supreme general with total control of the southern forces and fortifications.

A year after their victory, Kelyk turned his base into a mighty fortress, with a large keep now occupying the center of the courtyard. With the help of the wizard, he now had three working gold mines and over a hundred more towers covering the southern border, and more being built each week. A small village had cropped up around the main fortress that was filled with craftsmen, miners, and many more. The king had sent various princesses and noble women to court him, and he eventually found the woman of his dreams and married her.

Fifteen years after the great victory Kelyk is the wealthiest man in the kingdom with six children and a happy and loving marriage. The small village has grown to a mighty city and his thousands of towers are legendary, which have now spread throughout the whole kingdom keeping them all safe. Kelyk has also managed to broker a lasting peace with the barbarians. They now work together, teaching and sharing their resources and knowledge, with a very profitable trade route opened up between the two countries.

Kelyk lived happily ever after, having made the world a much better place. His legacy lives on for thousands of years, his people eventually opening up the age of enlightenment, a ten thousand year reign of peace, happiness, prosperity, and love across the whole world.

The End

Sneak Preview of Immortaland

And so it was that after thirty years of adventuring, leveling, learning, and becoming even more powerful, the mighty hero was able to manipulate time, open a portal, slay the guardian, defeat the evil king, and claim the all mighty book of knowledge for his own. After several more decades of diligent study, research, and praying, he was finally strong enough, pure enough, powerful enough and wise enough to create his very own magical kingdom with unlimited power. He named this kingdom IMMORTALAND, and he lived there forever more, happy as anyone could ever hope to be, making his kingdom stronger and better every chance he got! Immortaland has now gone exponential and is a mighty bastion of goodness that ensures the abundant existence of all that is good throughout all of space and time.

You say the magic words: "Immortaland, Immortaland, Immortaland"

You suddenly find yourself in a beautiful field filled with bright green grass and beautiful flowers of all descriptions. Blue, orange, red, and yellow butterflies flap in the warm breeze and the two suns are bright among puffy white clouds. The sky is a beautiful shade of blue. Looking down, you see yourself in a diamond circle, easily five feet wide. The gems sparkle under the noon day suns and in the golden road in which they are embedded.

Behind you, the golden road ends abruptly at the entrance to a beach paradise overflowing with yellow sand. Waves of pure clean water splash merrily against the sandy shore, inviting you to jump in and take a swim. Where the golden road turns into yellow sand, stand two beautiful smiling women. One has long flowing blonde hair and is wearing a tight red bikini, while the other has fiery red hair tied back in a diamond pony tail, sporting a yellow bikini studded with rubies. The red head, named Sandra, blows you a kiss, while the blonde, named Beverlyn, beckons for you to come and join them on the beach. You wave to them and then run into their welcoming embrace, giving each a passionate kiss on the lips. With a tinge of regret you tell them "Have some fun without me for a bit, I will be back shortly."

The look of sadness on their faces and their disappointed whimpering is too much to bear, so you raise your fist in the air, calling upon the magical powers that are everywhere in this land, and suddenly a clone of yourself appears, complete with golden armor and crown. Your clone gives you a knowing wink and then grabs each woman by the hand and starts heading for the beach. "Come on ladies, you can help me get out of this armor." The women giggle as the trio run to the beach.

Turning around, you see the golden brick road ending at the base of a massive fairy tale castle of diamond and pure white marble. There are four massive towers on each corner of the castle, and a great tower in the center, which reaches high into the puffy white clouds.

The great tower is enchanted with an un-breakable magical shield of power that extends one-hundred miles in all directions, including above and underneath the massive island. Each of the diamond and white marble corner towers is capped with turrets of solid gold that sparkle under the life giving suns. Each tower is equipped with their own unique set of deadly weapons, guardians, traps, enchantments, and defenses to keep the realm safe.

At the base of the castle are a magnificent assortment of rose bushes, orange trees, raspberry bushes, apple trees, and all sorts of other flowers, herbs, and fruit trees. All of the fruits and flowers are in full bloom, and stay that way throughout the years by the powerful magic emanating from the castle itself.

You can hear songbirds chirping merrily and can see many others flying through the air or sitting in the trees, their beauty a joy to behold. The birds here are magical, and have the effect of making you feel healthy and happy just by watching them and listening to their beautiful songs. This is also a favorite place for pets, animals, and magical creatures of the realm to get together and play in the bountiful gardens that surround the castle.

Looking around, you can see several great heroes from legends, stories, and from famous video games strolling along and looking quite heroic. You teleport over to them, slapping them a high five! You then recount some stories of your epic adventures together, bringing smiles all around. After a few fond memories you say goodbye, knowing that if any trouble should arise, that these heroes and all the other heroes located throughout Immortaland will fight to the death for your cause.

Ahead of you, the golden road ends at a large diamond door in the center of the castle. A fabulous sun of yellow diamonds decorates the center of the door, shining brightly, and emitting another, more powerful shield that protects everything within 100 feet of the castle.

Check out the rest of the story in book or audio book format on my website: www.LordHartRules.com

My Other Books and Audio Books

THE ANGEL'S BLESSING
HOLY PALADIN'S QUEST
BLAINE HART

SPELL MASTER
WIZARD'S QUEST
BLAINE HART

Blaine Hart
The Bard's Tale
A Mysterious Journey

THE SANDS OF TIME
THE ANGEL'S BLESSING
BLAINE HART

For A Special Treat, check out my

<u>AUDIO BOOKS</u>

Thanks for reading!

If you enjoyed this book a nice review would be greatly appreciated.

Check Out all My Books and Audio Books at:
www.LordHartRules.com

www.ingramcontent.com/pod-product-compliance
Lightning Source LLC
Chambersburg PA
CBHW082104090726
47910CB00008B/2592